PROM DATE

The first day of class of my high school career. I met the woman who would become my prom date and I had no idea. I was the only person in the English class early when Miss Amber walked in and said good morning. I said good morning, Miss Amber and she flashed the prettiest smile that I've ever seen in my young life.

Miss Amber is a voluptuous short haired brunette with glasses. When I saw her my heart skipped a beat and it was love at first sight. I was ready to learn anything that she wanted to teach me. I went home that day and told Heather that I saw the most beautiful woman in the world Miss Amber.

Heather said that is sweet that you have a crush on your teacher. I said I look forward to learning a lot in her class. It was still summer in Arlington, Texas where we all live and go to school. A week later when Miss Amber wore a very beautiful summer dress. I told her how amazing she looked in her dress and that in my opinion she was the most beautiful woman in the world. Miss Amber turned red and said thank you sweetheart that means a lot to hear you say that to me.

High School went by fast for me, before I knew it, I had a girlfriend before she dumped me just before prom to go with her dream date, the quarterback of the football team. That is when I had a crazy idea. I marched to Miss Amber's office knocked on the door. I was nervous as hell and shaking like a leaf. She said you can come on in.

I was sweating a little bit and ringing my hands. Miss Amber said have a seat, I sat down, and she smiled at me. She said I heard that your girlfriend broke up with you just before prom. I said oh yeah, it sucks but will you go to the prom with me Miss Amber.

I was thinking that she would say hell no and twice on Sunday. But to my surprise Miss Amber said I remember your first day of high school and our first class, you were an hour early. I said sorry about that, I wanted to learn. She said you have grown into a wonderful young man whom I adore.

So, I will be happy to be your date to your senior prom. My eyes doubled in size, and I said oh My god Miss Amber thank you so much for agreeing to be my date to the senior prom. She said you are very welcome, and I look forward to dancing with you all night. I said I look forward to it too.

I hugged Miss Amber tightly and she said oh wow you are very strong. I said sorry, I didn't mean to squeeze you so tight. I got a little excited. She said its ok I love your enthusiasm for our prom date.

Prom night the limousine that Heather ordered picked up Miss Amber and brought her to our house. I retrieved Miss Amber from the car and wow, I said you look amazing in that beautiful red evening gown.

I brought Miss Amber to meet my white mommy, Heather. She said it is finally nice to meet you Miss Amber, he talks about you all the time. Miss Amber giggled and said is that true. I said yeah, I think you are the most beautiful and intelligent woman ever.

Miss Amber said why thank you kindly, you raised such a gentleman, Heather. Miss Amber said I'm sure you want some pictures. I said she insist on it. I took Miss Amber to Heather's studio; she is a professional photographer.

Miss Amber said this looks so professional. Heather said it's my job and a passion of mine. I said sorry about all the pictures of me. Miss Amber said I love the pictures of you, you are so handsome. I said thank you Miss Amber. Heather was all set up and ready. She started taking pictures and more pictures of me holding Miss Amber.

It felt like a dream holding Miss Amber so close and intimate. Heather shocked us both when she said how about a little kiss on the lips, just a little peck. I said no Heather, you don't have to do that Miss Amber. She shocked me by saying what if I wanted to give you a peck on the lips.

I swallowed and then said ok. Miss Amber gave me a peck on the lips and Heather got the shot. I felt that kiss throughout my entire body and I thought wow. We finished the photo shoot then I took Miss Amber by the hand and helped her into the limousine.

We were driving along when Miss Amber took my hand and said you look so handsome tonight. I am proud to be your date to the senior prom. I said you look so pretty, and you have no idea how much taking the most beautiful girl in the world to the prom means to me.

Miss Amber smile broadly and patted my hand. We reached the prom site and I said wait let me open the door for you. I hopped out in my all-white tuxedo and ran around to open the door for Miss Amber.

I took her hand and helped her out of the limousine. We walked up and gave them our invitations to the prom. I walked into the prom thinking what's up bitches, I have a date and she is hot like fire.

I said hello to my buddies at the prom and a few ladies that I'm friends with. The prom started popping and everyone was on the dance floor dancing. I held Miss Amber while dancing. We were all smiles then I saw my ex-Angela with her new boyfriend making out like crazy.

Miss Amber said when we get back into the limousine, we are going to make out. I said really and Miss Amber said oh yeah. The thought of that made me fully aroused. I said oh no sorry about that Miss Amber.

Miss Amber held me closer and said I love it. I said oh my god you're so hot Miss Amber that is when she moaned into my ears and said oh wow that feels really big. I said thank you, Miss Amber. We were both grinding on each other, oh wow I couldn't believe what was happening.

Our harmonious lustful embrace was overwhelming and powerful to my entire being. I was drunk on lust for Miss Amber. Miss Amber said after you graduate, if you still want me, we can make love to each other in my apartment. I said I will always want you, Miss Amber. She said it is settled then after graduation, you come over and we will have amazing coitus with your big black penis inside of my white vagina.

I said that will be the best graduation present ever. Miss Amber said I'm so wet with anticipation. I said are you wet right now, Miss Amber said very wet. I said you are the woman of my dreams and she smiled then kissed me on the cheek.

After the prom, we held hands and walked to the limousine. We put up the privacy screen then Miss Amber kissed me on the lips. We kissed like crazy with our hands all over each other. Miss Amber started rubbing my cock that's when I massaged her big natural breasts.

Miss Amber ended up on top of me. We were kissing like crazy. I grabbed her big juicy ass and squeezed it properly.

The limousine came to a stop. We stopped what we were doing and sat upright. The driver put down the privacy screen and said we are at your Apartment complex Miss Amber. We hugged tightly and whispered sweet nothings into each other's ears before saying our goodbyes.

I went home high on lust for Miss Amber. Heather was waiting up for me. She asked how was the prom? I said it was amazing, Miss Amber and I made out in the limousine, Heather then high fived me saying that was great honey. I'm happy for you giving me a great big hug.

Senior finals were up next, and I was studying so hard in the library. I didn't notice Miss Amber sneaking up on me. She whispered in my ears, hey sexy man what are you up to with all those big textbooks. I turned to look at her and she smiled at me.

I said what are you doing here. She said I was passing by when I saw you studying, I thought, I'd come say hi. I got up and hugged her tight. Miss Amber said I can't wait until you graduate, there will be a lot of fireworks in my apartment. She winked at me and said later sweetheart.

I went back to studying but I couldn't concentrate. I called it a day and went home. I kept studying as the days ticked by towards graduation. I was very happy a week later when I passed all of my finals with and A grade.

I was very happy; Heather was very happy too. I texted Miss Amber that I passed all of my classes and I'm on track to graduate in May. Miss Amber replied, a smart stud. I replied thank you goddess.

Graduation day, I put on my cap and gown along with my honors tassel. I came downstairs and went to the studio where Heather was waiting. I took all the pictures that she wanted me to take then we took off to the graduation ceremony.

I went with my fellow graduates and got seated with our name tags on our chairs. I waited for my name to be called. I was excited for my name to be called I went up there and collected my diploma from the principal then I got a hug from Miss Amber in front of the entire sea of people.

After the graduation festivities. I think I took a picture with everyone there. I loved taking pictures with Miss Amber. She told me that she is very happy that my favorite student and future lover is now a graduate from the senior high school that I now teach.

Heather asked Miss Amber to take a few pictures of us. Miss Amber was very eager to take pictures of me and my white mommy. Miss Amber said can you send me some of those, she gave my mom her phone number.

Heather took me to dinner at a fancy restaurant. She gave me a box with a present in it, when I opened it, it was a Rolex. I said thank you Heather and she gave me a peck on the lips, hugging me tightly. We talked like normal and had a great dinner.

A few days later, a male model bailed on Heather for a photo shoot. So, she asked me to model some male swim wear for her. She told me that I had a great body and I'll pay you for your time. I said ok and I went to put on the swim trunks. Heather was wearing a sexy vest and a short skirt doing the photo shoot. Everything was going fine for about an hour when Heather's tits popped out.

Heather said oops sorry honey, you are not supposed to see your white mommies' titties. I said its ok you have big, wonderful breast and Heather laughed out loud. We were going to start up the photo shoot again when Heather said ah, your penis is bulging.

I said sorry about that Heather, I see big boobs and I get hard. She said let's just wait 5 minutes and it will go away. 5 minutes later and I was still hard as a rock. Heather said how about I give you a hand job to get rid of your erection. I said that would be great Heather, it will definitely go down then.

I took my penis out for Heather, she said oh wow that is a very big penis. I said thanks as Heather started to stroke my erection thoroughly. I moaned oh Heather this feels so good baby. She said I like stroking your big penis, it's so wonderful, do you mind if your white mommy stimulates your penis with her mouth.

I said I don't mind go for it, Heather started licking my penis up and down the shaft and oh man did it feel great. She proceeded to put my penis in her mouth and stimulated it properly. Heather knew how to really stimulate a penis properly; I was high on lust. I said I love you Heather as she blew my mind beyond what I thought was possible.

Heather stopped and said would you like to have sexual intercourse with your white mommy and make us both feel wonderful. I shook my head up and down yes as Heather smiled broadly.

Heather led me by the penis to the bed in her photography studio. She said kiss me and I kissed her with a lot of passion. Next, she said suck my melons baby. I grabbed her big titties and suckled her breast until I could suckle no more.

She said take my red panties off and stick your big black penis inside my white vagina. I was very happy to remove her red panties and I smelt them, it was wet and intoxicating to my sense of wonder.

I held my penis and Heather said wow your big. She said you are going to have to force that in me, it's not going to go in normally, your white mommy hasn't had sex in a while. I held her hips and forcefully penetrated Heather's wet vagina.

Oh wow, I couldn't believe I was balls deep inside Heather and she fucking liked it a lot. I started sliding my black penis in and out of Heather's warm vagina. The pleasure was immense both of us were moaning like crazy as I fucked her pussy well. Heather said oh god honey I'm coming on your big penis. I looked down and saw a lot of cream on my cock shaft.

I said oh Heather as I gave her more of my love. I kissed her as she held the back of my neck. I gave Heather long deep hard strokes in harmonic unison until I felt that god like feeling before an orgasm, it hit me and I feel the love all over my body, it was fucking electrifying.

I held Heather and she wrapped her legs around me holding me tight. When our pleasure high wore off, Heather said that was amazing sweetheart, I really needed that from you at this moment in time. I said it was my pleasure to give you what you needed.

After a week of making love to Heather, once or twice a day. I had to tell her about Miss Amber. I said Heather we need to talk and she said oh no. I said don't be mad but Miss Amber invited me to come to her apartment to have sexual intercourse with her.

Heather said that's fine, we are still going to have sexual intercourse, right. I said hell yeah, I love penetrating my white mommy and giving it to her strong. Heather said oh yeah that's my black boy. I love when you talk dirty to your white mommy.

We hugged and kissed, Heather said I'm glad that we are still going to be lovers. I don't care who you fuck as long as you stay in between my sweet white thighs, we are all good. I kissed her and said I'm never giving you up, I love you Heather and she said I love you too, honey.

Heather said I'll let you rest up the rest of the week for Miss Amber. The night I was going to go over to her apartment. Heather watched me get ready with a smile on her pretty face. We hugged goodbye and Heather said enjoy Miss Amber's vagina. I laughed out loud and so did Heather.

I drove over to Miss Amber's apartment. I rang the doorbell and she came to the door in an open robe. I could see her big tits and manicure black bush. Her look overwhelmed me with lust and passion for her body. She took me by the hand and led me to the bedroom.

Miss Amber took all of my clothes off my naked body kissing every inch of me. She dropped her robe and we crawled into bed naked. We held each other lovingly and kissed each other. I suckled her breasts then kissed my way down to her clit. I sucked on her clit and fingered her cunt driving her wild with pleasure.

Miss Amber said come stick your dick in my mouth. I want to suck my first black cock. I pushed my black cock into her warm mouth, Miss Amber sucked my cock and stroked it really good. I fucking loved it then she stopped and said time to penetrate me baby.

I held my black cock at her white vagina. I gave her my dagger of love strong. She screamed with pleasure and pain. I held her ankles and slowly fucked her. I moaned oh Miss Amber, you are my favorite teacher. She said I love your big black cock my favorite student.

I saw Miss Amber's eyes roll back in her head as I fucked her harder. I saw her reward my cock with her pussy cream. Miss Amber said lay back let me ride you baby. I laid back and Miss Amber mounted me. I squeezed her big tits as she slid up and down my black pole. She moaned, oh god so good, I'm cumming on your big black pole again baby look. I looked at my cock and saw more cream sliding down.

I said I want you doggie baby. Miss Amber got on all fours. I mounted her from behind giving her a full dose of black cock. I smacked her juicy big ass and took her hard. She screamed and creamed as I hammered her sweet white pussy while her ass jiggled off my hips.

I moaned oh Miss Amber as I delivered the winning touchdown of sperm in her tight little cunt. Miss Amber said oh yeah baby fill me with your warm joy. I massaged her ass and said that was worth 4 years of waiting. Miss Amber said oh yeah it was baby.

We lay beside each other smiling and holding hands. We fell asleep together and woke up together. Miss Amber was watching me as I woke up. She said good morning my handsome chocolate lover. I said good morning Miss Amber. She said I love hearing you call me Miss Amber. I smiled and kissed her.

Miss Amber reached for my cock then said oh wow its hard and we fucked last night. She said I can't waste this opportunity, stick it in baby. I got on top of Miss Amber and penetrated her. She was wet and ready as I filled her with my black bone.

I gave it to her fast and hard. She held the small of my back and took it like a champ. I hammered the shit out of her. Miss Amber creamed my penis a few times before I filled her up with fresh morning sperm.

We kissed and held each other smiling, enjoying our time together. I said I remember the day in your class when I turned 18, you wore a short red skirt and white top. I had an erection the whole class. Miss Amber said oh my god you remember that I was the happiest girl in school that day.

When I saw you in that skirt and your sweet white thighs. I almost died of pleasure. Miss Amber said I was wet the whole class looking at the bulge in your pants. I saw you looking at my bulge and it warmed my heart with lust for you.

A few weeks into my sleeping with Miss Amber, I snuck her into the house. Everything went fine, I fucked the shit out of Miss Amber that night. I was on top of her kissing her, with her arms and legs wrapped around me. When my white mommy came to my room naked and caught me with my cock still in Miss Amber. Heather said oh crap, I didn't know you had company. I got off of Miss Amber. Heather saw her and said hi Miss Amber.

Miss Amber said why are you naked, are you fucking him too. Heather said yeah, his white mommy is addicted to his big black cock what can I say. I said I'm sorry Miss Amber, I'm not giving her up.

Miss Amber said its ok, I don't want you too, I love kinky stuff. Heather said sweetie your cock's hard again. Miss Amber saw it and her eyes got wide, she looked at Heather said you want to ride his dirty black cock that he just took out of me. Heather said fuck yeah, I thought you would never ask.

Heather ran to my bed held my dirty black pole and slid her white pussy down it quickly. I squeezed her big fucking titties as she fucked my cock. Miss Amber said oh my god this is so fucking hot, a white mommy riding her black sons big black cock.

Heather moaned as she lubricated my cock with her orgasm. Miss Amber held Heather's pretty face and kissed her passionately with reciprocation from Heather, which caused me to ejaculate all of my warm sperm into Heather's wonderful cunt.

The end

www.ingramcontent.com/pod-product-compliance
Lightning Source LLC
LaVergne TN
LVHW052115160826
845678LV00015B/3575

* 9 7 9 8 3 5 3 2 6 9 6 6 3 *